The Powerful Penelope Pym
Brian D. Campbell

Printed in the United States of America
First Printing, 2023

ISBN 979-8-9873549-2-6 (Paperback)
ISBN 979-8-9873549-3-3 (Mobi eBook)

Red Cliff Press
PO Box 371
New Boston, NH 03070

For Those Who Wish to be Seen

I see you and I appreciate you.

An illustrative interpretation of the Vermeer Windmill in Pella, Iowa. Credit to
Kashaf Mehsania of Internative Labs.

Preface

I'd thought about naming this memoir, *The Diary of Penelope Pym*, and then maybe adding something more descriptive, like, *How I Met My Husband, and Nearly Killed Him*, but that seemed a little too cliché and perhaps a bit too dramatic. However, that doesn't make it any less honest.

The thought of just leaving the second part off seemed better, but not original enough. Plus, this is more than just a peek inside my diary. It's quite specific, and I'll be adding a lot of storytelling and narrating along the way.

After far more self-deliberation than I had ever imagined, I went with something completely unexpected and perhaps even illogical. But it's *my* memoir, so I can write it and name it however I choose. I chose, *The Powerful Penelope Pym*.

As you read the entries and my added commentary about them, you'll learn that the bold nickname comes from my father. Thanks, dad, for making me believe in my super powers, and for teaching me how to use them properly.

I'm going to share very specific pieces of my life-long diary that were chosen because they all include passages related to my eventual husband, Evan. This memoir is a coming of age tale with a heavy splash of romance and, if you're a little twisted like me, a tiny dash of comedy.

I'll be telling the story of how my oldest friend and sometimes enemy—the very same man that I've loved since I was in pigtails—eventually, after years of agony for both of us, became the absolute and undeniable love of my life.

I'll also be mixing in commentary about my own specific journey into adulthood from a romantic and even professional perspective. I'm sharing how I've changed as I learned and matured over the years.

The idea of writing a memoir came to me a few months after Evan and I were engaged. I decided to go back and read our story, as I had documented it over the years in my diary. If I worked hard enough, I could have it ready as a wedding present for my beloved husband.

What I read in my diary was nothing short of hilarious, or terrifying—depending on the reader's perspective.

At first glance, I'd considered locking the pages into a vault, so my poor fiancé could never see them and possibly change his mind about our wedding. But then, it occurred to me that if we had made it this far, after all that we'd put each other through, we were definitely destined to be together forever. Plus, some of this stuff is just too good to hide away.

My poor, poor, Evan. You must know by now, no matter what you read in the coming pages, my heart was always in the right place. It always belonged to you and no other. Please accept my love, along with my sincerest apologies.

Chapter 1

July 14, 2001

Dear Diary,

Today was literally the best day of my life. Well, it didn't really start that way. Evan Milan, the boy who lives across the street—we're gonna be talking about him a lot—was playing football with his stupid best friend, Trevor.

I wanted to play, because I wanted to show Evan that I wasn't just some dumb girl who liked to watch the boys play football. That's what all the other girls do—especially my best friend, Scarlett. They watch the boys play football and talk about them and laugh as loud as they can, so maybe the boys will notice that they're watching and talking about them.

Well, I'm not like those girls. Except Scarlett, we're a lot alike, but sometimes she's like the other girls and I wish she wasn't.

I knew I could play football and I wanted Evan to know that. Evan said I could play, but Trevor didn't want me to. Evan said he didn't care and he let me play.

I was on Evan's team and I didn't know what to do, but when we got into the huddle, Evan said he was going to give me the ball first. He said they would never believe I would get the ball, and I would be wide open. I didn't know what wide open means, but I didn't care. Evan was letting me play and even giving me the ball.

Evan yelled, "Hike!" and all the boys ran. I just stood there, all by myself. That's what wide open means. There was no one near me. Evan tossed the ball underhanded to me and I caught it.

Evan yelled, "Run!" but before I even knew anything, stupid Trevor tackled me, hard, and everything went black. He basically knocked me out in front of everyone.

By the time I knew where I was, I could hear Evan yelling at Trevor and Trevor saying, "That's why girls don't play football."

I wanted to cry, but I didn't. I waited till I got home to cry. I didn't want Evan to see me cry and I didn't want stupid Trevor to know he hurt me. I just went home as fast as I could go.

So that was the bad part of the day. This is the best part. This is the great part.

After I was home for a while and feeling much better, Evan came over. He rang our doorbell and my dad answered the door. My dad saw me crying when I got home and I told him I got hurt playing football with Evan. My dad was pretty mad, but I told him it wasn't Evan's fault.

My dad gave Evan the look of death, but Evan didn't get scared. He asked my dad if he could talk to me. He said he wanted to see if I was okay. My dad was impressed and said that was pretty thoughtful and he let Evan in.

Evan came and sat with me on the couch and watched TV with me for an hour. He asked if I was okay and I told him I was fine. We sat together the whole time.

Evan and I have been friends since preschool, but now I think we're more than friends. I think I might love Evan.

OKAY BYE!

I think I read this entry a thousand times and it made me laugh more with each pass. This was the first entry in my diary that was all about Evan, and it's quite a doozy. And, for the record, I wasn't knocked unconscious by Trevor. That was a little extra drama from a nine-year-old with an overactive imagination.

The image of nine-year-old Evan sitting in silence with me on the couch as I smiled from ear to ear had been permanently burned into my brain. I remember it like it was yesterday. It was adorable, awkward, and the most wonderful thing that had ever happened to me at that time in my life. That was the day I fell in love with the only person I've ever been in love with.

Sweet little Evan was brave enough to face my father and check on me. His chivalry had swept me off my tiny feet and he topped it off by staying with me for two whole episodes of *Lizzie McGuire*—my hero!

Evan and I have basically grown up together. He lived across the street and our families were very, very close. Our older brothers, Bradley and Thomas, were the same age as each other, both three years ahead of us, and they played football together. They were football stars, actually, in a town that put a premium on high school football talent.

Our older brothers were best friends, and legends—just like our fathers. Our dads played football together, too, and then, when they became fathers of boys, they coached football together.

We all actually still live in the same football-loving town and we love our town nearly as much as we love each other. I don't believe any of us will ever move.

So, what's the name of this wonderful Midwestern paradise? It's the one-and-only, Pella, Iowa.

Yes, that Pella—home to The Pella Corporation—famous for Pella Windows and Doors. We're so much more than that though. Our city is positively beautiful.

A better, but perhaps lesser known description of our town is, America's Dutch treasure. Pella comes complete with brick walkways, an authentic Dutch canal, and picturesque windmills. People come to our Tulip Festival from all over the world. We welcome the big crowds, but we still hold firm to our small town appeal.

Evan and I grew up on Lake Red Rock, outside of downtown. My parents were high school sweethearts, so were Evan's parents, and the four were close friends. It seems half of the parents in Pella were high school sweethearts.

Not a whole lot ever changes here. Friends and neighbors stay close for a long, long time. And since our families were so close, Evan and I spent a lot of parties, cookouts, and football games together.

My mother was the classic cheerleader type, complete with a homecoming queen's crown. She was the town beauty. You can imagine her excitement on the day I was born.

She had given my father his boy to mold in his own football toting image—and mold he did. With my arrival, she finally had a protégé of her own, and for years, she dressed me in perfect, pretty, pink dresses and pigtails—with glee.

By the time I'd started the second grade, I knew that none of that stuff was for me. I loved books, exploring the woods in our backyard, swimming in the lake nearby, and I absolutely hated it when someone dared to tell me how cute I was.

I was nothing like my mother, and it nearly broke her heart. She tried and tried, but I resisted her every attempt to shape me in any way. Our relationship was…complicated.

At nine years old, I'd began to realize I was a completely different kind of kid. I only had a few friends, Scarlett being the closest, and I generally kept to myself.

I'd read for hours, alone in the woods or in my room. The only time I would venture out to play with the other neighborhood kids was when Scarlett got bored and came to get me—or when Evan was around.

Thankfully, he always made sure I was seen and included in whatever games he and the other kids were playing.

The other kids would resist, but Evan was their ringleader and they tended to go along with whatever he wanted. Evan has been looking out for me my entire life, and, of course, I adored him for it. It took him a while to feel the same way, but we'll get into that later.

Though Evan had my back with the neighborhood kids, I didn't know at the time that the adoration wasn't completely mutual. His father had to constantly tell him to look out for me and to play with me. There were times, I'm sure, when he'd wished he could ignore me the same way all the other kids did, but his parents wouldn't allow it.

Looking back on my childhood, the only person who I believe really understood me was my father. When I'd started resisting my mother's urge to put me in dresses, he would take me shopping for school clothes that I'd actually wear.

When my mother would constantly ask me why I stayed cooped up in my room reading when all the other kids were playing outside, he would check on me and stroke my hair while I read. He said my love of reading was one of my many super powers. That, and never being afraid to be me, no matter who didn't like it.

When I came home crying after the football incident with Trevor, he stayed with me until I felt better. That was when he gave me the nickname he calls me to this very day. That was the day I became known to my father as The Powerful Penelope Pym.

Chapter 2

August 29, 2003

Dear Diary,

Monday is going to be the first day of junior high. Scarlett and Evan are both super excited about that, but that's only because he's on the football team and she made the cheer squad.

Woopty doo! I'm not excited AT ALL.

Scarlett told me if I really wanted Evan to look at me and see more than the little girl that lives across the street, I should try out for cheerleading. I said there's no way in heckle that I could ever be a cheerleader, and I meant it. Sorry, Scarlett.

"Rah Rah Rah! Let's go TEAM! Look at my pompoms and my tiny skirt!" Ummmm, no. Not for me. No, thank you.

Scarlett and I spent the entire summer hanging out with the beautiful Evan and his idiot best friend, Trevor—sadly, but once football and cheer practice started last week, they all abandoned me. That's fine. I have a pile of books to read from my dad, and though it was amazing to be around Evan all summer, I don't think I could stand another day of Trevor drooling over Scarlett.

I guess I must have seemed a little mopey at first, when they were gone, because my mom was bugging me and telling me I should try out for cheer, or something else. Ya, right mom. Something else? We both know, to you, there is no something else. Also, FYI—I am not your mini me. Sorry mommy.

My dad took a more awesome approach, like he always does. He told me to forget about all of that stuff and just be me. He said as long as I keep reading my books and being true to myself, someday, I might save the world, or something.

Oh, dad. Why should I save the world? Does the world deserve to be saved? I think the best thing I could do for the world, or, more appropriately, for the morons living on it, is to let them fail miserably. People actually learn a lesson when they fail—sometimes.

Planet Earth would be a lot better off if people like me did nothing at all to help the idgits living on it—and destroying it. So, by doing nothing to save humanity, I would be doing the world a huge favor.

Besides, when you try to tell people to stop doing something stupid, they just want to do it more and more. So, daddy dearest, even if I could, I would not try to save the world.

But, enough of that.

Like I was saying, Trevor—still a jerk—flirted with Scarlett almost every day, ALL SUMMER LONG. But she's really not into him, THANK GOD! I don't know who she likes, and that's fine, as long as it's not Evan. Evan is mine, and she knows that. I just wish Evan knew that. He will, some day.

Trevor was constantly ogling Scarlett and talking about how she was already developing in the chest area, and then he said I looked like a skinny nine-year-old boy. I'm sure that didn't encourage Evan to like me the way I like him— Thanks Trevor. You're such a great friend.

In case you forgot, I HATE TREVOR!

Anyway, I'll be savoring every minute of freedom this weekend until school starts on Tuesday. The good news is, I'll get to see Evan again, FINALLY. The bad news is, his shadow, Trevor, will probably be stuck to him like a used-up piece of gum stuck to the bottom of your shoe, just like the rest of the slime and filth that gathers there.

Evan will be mine this year. And I won't have to prance around in a teeny little skirt to get his attention. Evan is a better person than that. But thanks for the idea, Scarlett. Have fun hanging out with the POOPular girls.

This was the summer before we entered the sixth grade—before everything had begun to change. I was positively obsessed with Evan at the time and we were good friends. The closeness of our foursome that I had mentioned in my diary entry was accurate—we spent almost the entire summer together. We were the fab four.

I was still optimistic about my chances with Evan, but he was far less enthusiastic about anything more than a friendship. At least by then he was spending time with me because he wanted to, and not because his parents were encouraging him to. Still, I was too young and full of hope to see the writing on the wall. We were going into junior high school from completely different angles. And our differences were about to stand out much more prominently.

My three friends were gifted in ways that I simply was not. Evan and Trevor were great athletes and they made the junior high football team as sixth graders. That was a rare feat. And, because of their talents, and their legacy, they were destined for godhood.

Scarlett was popular and beautiful—even at eleven. And, sadly, Trevor was right about me. I looked like a skinny nine-year-old boy. Thankfully, that changed, but not until several years later.

I still spent weekends with my three friends, when they didn't have games to play or cheer for. We were still the fab four for a short while. Trevor still drooled over Scarlett, and she still ignored him. I still dreamt about Evan and he still only saw me as a friend.

But, when we were at school, we were clearly in two different social classes. They ran with the top of the popularity food chain and I hung around with the kids who wished they were one of them. That is, I hung around with those kids when they would have me.

By that time, I was developing a bit of an attitude problem. I had discovered, or at least I thought I had, that I was the smartest person in the room—every room.

I corrected other students in class. I corrected my teachers in class. I corrected the principal when they told me to stop correcting the teachers and other students in class. And then, after a call home from school, I corrected my parents when they told me to stop correcting *literally everyone*—especially the principal—all the time.

Like the ridiculous comment in my diary entry about being merciful and allowing humanity make its mistakes and eventually die off had implied, I was convinced that I knew everything. The rest of the world was just too clueless to waste my self-conceived, eleven-year-old brilliance on.

That was me, at eleven years old. I was as abrasive as sandpaper. Fortunately, for the rest of the world, they were still blissfully ignorant of what was coming for them.

Yes, it got worse.

Chapter 3

April 25, 2004

Dear Diary,

'm grounded for two weeks. YAY! THANKS MOM! I mean, it's not like I have anywhere to go or anything, so it really doesn't matter much.

Why am I being punished? I got kicked off the math team for calling Mr. Morin, the coach, *Mr. Moron*.

You know, the math team? The team I only joined because my mother made me? Yeah, that math team.

I guess my friend, Leia, the only semi-smart person on the team, and the rest of the brainless wonders will have to geek out for the rest of the year without the only member of their precious team who could actually calculate equations. Good luck with just *Mr. Moron* to guide you.

Also, for the record, and as stated above, Mr. Morin *is* officially a moron, and everyone knows that. I was just the only one who wasn't afraid to tell him that. So, technically, I'm being punished for telling the truth. That seems totally fair to me.

Enough of that. I really don't care. On a much more personal and slightly more pitiful note, Leia has officially replaced Scarlett as my best friend. On an even more pitiful note, Leia is actually my only friend. At least Leia will never stab me in the back—so, that's good. Bonus for me.

What happened with Scarlett? I thought you would never ask. It seems that Scarlett has grown a second face. One face—the pretty cheerleadery one that we all know and love—was constantly encouraging me to keep hope alive that Evan and I would be together, and that we were meant to be together, and BLAH! BLAH! BLAH! LIE! LIE! LIE!

And the second face—the nasty, lying, demony one that she hides from the world—was madly in love with Evan and trying to take him for herself. BEHIND MY BACK!

So, needless to say, I shall be telling tales of Penelope and Scarlett adventures no longer. Perhaps I should be sad about that. Maybe I will be, once I'm done being angry. Let's say, maybe in one-hundred years, M'kay? M'kay.

Evan has not fallen for her just yet. THANK GOD! And he still talks to me, sometimes, but we hardly spend any actual time together any more. I want to be angry with him about that, but I don't know why. He hasn't really done anything wrong. He hasn't changed since like, forever. He's still perfect in every way. Besides, it's not like I've ever had the courage to tell him how I feel. I just wish he knew, somehow. WHY CAN'T HE JUST KNOW?

That's all I have for today. My favorite parent—my dad, not the former cheerleading beauty queen who birthed me—wants to take me for a ride with him to the store, or something, to help relieve some of my boredom. I bet he'll buy me a book. I bet I'll have to hide it from the other less-loving parent.

Love you, dad. TTFN

A few weeks before the end of sixth grade it had been brought to my attention by one of Scarlett's far more popular friends that Scarlett liked Evan.

Though I played it pretty cool, or maybe I didn't, as documented in my diary entry, I was crushed. Scarlett and I had been best friends for as long as I could remember. And though heavy crushes on the same objects of affection have been challenging the fabric of best friendships since the dawn of time, and most friendships recover from such tragedies, this one had proven to be a permanent deal breaker for Scarlett and me.

Evan and I still see Scarlett all the time, as you'll learn later. She still has a huge role to play in this memoir. Sadly, however, our close friendship never fully recovered from the revelation that she was keeping such a poisonous secret from me for who knows how long. She always knew how madly in love

I was with Evan and she never mentioned having her own feelings for him.

I'm not sure if it was just the fact that she dared to fall for the same boy as me, or if it was just the natural order of things—we clearly went our separate ways in junior high school and beyond—but either way, Scarlett and I are merely cordial with each other today.

Scarlett is much more like my mother than I am. She ran with the cool crowd, and I was part of the math team. I was part of the math team, that is, until they kicked me off the team for calling our coach, Mr. Morin, *Mr. Moron*, right to his face.

All of the kids called him that, behind his back. It was a joke, really. To the rest of the kids, it was just a play on words. But to twelve-year-old Penelope—the girl who believed she was smarter and therefore superior to the mere mortals of the world—it was reality. He was a moron. Everyone was a moron, except my father, of course.

My mother was furious when she found out that I had been so disrespectful to our teacher-coach. I'm fairly certain getting kicked off the math team didn't bother her all that much. Academics were never really her thing. But hearing from my principal about how I'd treated Mr. Morin definitely did.

I'm shocked that the incident didn't lead to more encouragement to join the cheer team—the door was open for that—but she had given up on that dream long before the *Mr. Moron* incident.

Still, my presence on the math team was actually her idea. She had never recovered from my absolute refusal to be involved with cheer or the pep squad, and she insisted I get involved with something. So, I reluctantly joined the math team, which was short-lived, but not a total loss for me. I managed to meet Leia, who became my best and only friend. Leia and I are still close today.

My father was upset with me, too, but he didn't come down on me nearly as hard as my mother had—he almost never punished me for anything, actually. And this time, because I told my father everything, he knew I was hurting over the Scarlett situation. So, he took it especially easy on me.

We had this ritual that we followed when I was sad. He'd invite me to go with him on whatever errand he might be running—a trip to the hardware or grocery store, or wherever. If I joined him, we would always swing by the bookstore downtown on Main Street and I'd get a new book.

My mother had actually complained a few times about the constant gift giving. This time, when my father asked me to come with him for a short reprieve from my punishment, she specifically told him that I was not to come home with anything in hand—a new book in particular.

When we got home with my new book, my dad told me in the car to go straight to my room with it and not to mention anything about it to my mother.

Our agreement seemed like a good plan, but my mother was waiting for us at the door inside the house. I was sent to my room without my new copy of Cornelia Funke's, *Inkheart,* which had been confiscated immediately as contraband.

My poor father got it almost as bad as I had when she found out about the *Mr. Moron* thing. And, to this day, I still don't know what ever happened to that book.

Chapter 4

May 30, 2004

Dear Diary,

E arlier tonight I was sitting on a blanket in our back yard with a flashlight reading my newest book, *Saving Francesca*, by Melina Marchetta.

My original plan was to get a good look at the comet LINEAR with the telescope I got for Christmas last year, but NO SUCH LUCK!

I'm sure it was up there somewhere, at least that's what they said on the news, but my sad attempt to locate it failed and I gave up. I bet I could have found it if I cared enough to try harder, but I didn't. So, I didn't.

Plus, I mean, I'm sure someone in Iowa who is an even bigger nerd than me is going to get a good image of the thing on their much better telescope and then snap a picture of it. They'll be so super proud of themselves and post their awesome picture all over the internet. And then, I can just look at that anytime I want, RIGHT? Right.

So, I decided to go with Plan B and read my new book.

There I was, reading my book, minding my own business, when guess who came walking over from across the street?

DING, DING! You guessed it. It was Evan. We haven't talked in so long, and now that school's out, I didn't think I'd see very much of him at all.

Well, my whole family is actually going over to his house for a barbeque tomorrow for Memorial Day, but I had no clue if he was even gonna be there. He's way too cool these days to be found at family functions. Guess what though, HE SAID HE'LL BE THERE! So, I get two straight days of Evan. And it's not even my birthday.

Well, anyway, I was reading and he walked up and shouted, "Hey, Pen! What's up?"

Pen? I know, right? Pen Pym? No Evan, just no.

He was too cute to be corrected, so I just let the *Pen* thing slide, for now. I'll crush that later, if it becomes a thing. Also, I've been called worse by far less attractive people.

On with the story. Evan noticed the light in my back yard and said he figured it was me, so he thought he'd come over just to say hi. He said we haven't talked in a while, AND HE MISSED ME!

I told him that I had been wondering when we might ever hang out again, playing it all cool, while my heart nearly pounded out of my chest. He said he would make sure to come over more often to just hang out and talk.

I asked him about Scarlett, the traitor. I didn't call her that out loud, I just thought it. I assumed he knew that she and I weren't best of friends anymore. He knew. I'm sure he knew why too.

Then, he said the greatest thing I'd ever heard him say since way back when we both learned how to talk. "I'm not real sure how she's doing. To be honest, I've been avoiding her."

I played it cool some more and asked, "What do you mean? Why would you avoid her?"

"Well, you know she likes me, right?"

OH I KNOW, EVAN!

I just nodded and let him tell me more.

"She makes me kind of uncomfortable. She's, like, aggressive and stuff."

Just more nodding from me. I was getting a little nervous about what he might tell me next. What the heck did she do to him? And then he blew me away and answered my prayers with what he said.

"I don't really like her that much. I don't really think I'm ready for all of that with her. I mean, I've never even kissed a girl before."

HALLELUJAH!

Sorry, didn't mean to get all religious there, but those were the most beautiful words these ears have ever heard.

One, Evan is a sweet guy and not ready for the *aggressive* tendencies of one Miss Scarlett. Two, he came to me to talk about all of that. He trusted me with some pretty personal stuff. EVAN TRUSTED ME!

I told him he could come over and hide out with me anytime he needed to get away from Scarlett, because there's no way she'd be coming over here anytime soon.

We talked there until forever. We talked about everything. When he left he told me how great it was to just hang out and talk with me. Kiss? Sadly, no kiss. Maybe soon. Remember, Scarlett is the aggressive one.

I'm the one who has his heart. SO SORRY SCARLETT! NOT!

Evan kept his promise and came over to visit me several times that summer. We never went anywhere beyond my house or my yard, but we spent a lot of time chatting about things. He was more open with me than he'd ever been.

I learned so much about Evan during the summer of 2004—his taste in girls, the pressure his father was putting on him with sports, what he wanted his future to look like, the fact that he wanted to be married someday and have kids. It was about as much information and life philosophy that a twelve-year-old could form at such a tender age. And most of it didn't change when he became an adult.

We developed a pretty tight bond that summer, but there were some rough times to come, I'm afraid. We're getting closer to that.

My good friend, Leia, tried to warn me every time I had mentioned to her that Evan and I had talked. She saw the inevitable and I was too intoxicated with infatuation to see any reason at all to be cautious or concerned.

"Be careful with him," she would say. "I wouldn't trust him. He'll break your heart. Why doesn't he ever invite you to hang out with him and his friends?"

She would tell me about seeing Evan with his inner circle at the movies or at the mall. Scarlett was always there and when Scarlett noticed Leia looking at them, she would kick things up a notch and hang all over Evan and laugh loudly—always checking to make sure Leia saw the way they were carrying on.

I didn't care. I got to see Evan regularly, and in those moments, I had him all to myself. He was opening up with me. He was showing me who he was—and I was loving every minute of it.

Chapter 5

July 3, 2006

Dear Diary,

Evan didn't come to our Fourth of July party today with his family. I'm sure if I had bothered to ask him if he were coming, he would have just said he had other plans. He may have even led me to believe that he was doing something with his new high school football friends—something far more exciting than hanging around with me and the rest of our boring relatives.

I'm sure he would say something like that, if I cared to ask, but the truth is that he was spending time with his new girlfriend, far away from here. Far away, because there was no chance he would have ever brought her to a party at my house.

Remember when I was complaining for a few weeks about how Evan hasn't come to see me all summer? Well, it wasn't because he's been too busy doing other things. It wasn't because he's going to be on the varsity football team as a freshman next year and everyone in our high school already worships him.

Well, almost everyone. I'm sure our brothers, Bradley and Thomas, both seniors, are going to pound on him pretty good at practice—and I hope they do. Word is they've already been teasing him and Trevor about how much they're going to. I wish I could help them—the older boys, NOT the younger boys.

The real reason Evan has been ignoring me is because he's actually with Scarlett now—they're an item—and although he's man enough to play football with giants, he's not actually man enough to tell me to my face that he's dating my former best friend.

I know I would have probably been upset with him if he had told me in person. I'm sure I would have shown some disgust and given him a hard time, but we're friends—well, we were friends.

I would have eventually realized that he and I as a thing wasn't ever going to happen, and then I would do the right thing and support him and his horrible choice of a girlfriend. I would still be a good friend, and tell him he's making an enormous mistake. A HUGE MISTAKE. That's part of what friends do. But then, it would be up to him to do whatever he felt was right.

I like to think that's how it would have gone down, but who knows? I guess no one will ever know. I guess I lost one of my best friends because he's a coward and a liar. That's two for two, I guess. I'm so happy they have each other though.

I've had time to think about it all. Leia told me a couple days ago, so I knew he wasn't coming today. I'm not being all pouty about it. I won't throw a fit, or cry, or be all dramatic about it.

Leia has been pretty awesome about the whole thing. She never once said I told you so. She's not like that. She keeps telling me that high school starts soon and we can put all the junior high drama behind us. We get a chance to start fresh and meet some new, older friends.

Leia has way more optimism than I do, but she means well. I'm pretty sure high school is going to be exactly like junior high. It'll be filled with imbeciles—slightly older imbeciles, but imbeciles all the same.

My dad tells me that one day all of this will be a fond memory and I won't even think about any of the drama at all. I'll be on to bigger and better things.

"The Powerful Penelope Pym will look back on this moment and laugh about it."

I can't wait.

Don't expect me to be talking to you about Evan any longer. I'm moving on—to bigger and better things.

The end of junior high was a pretty tough time for me, despite the diary entry statements that I was moving on. I was not nearly as composed as I had pretended to be in my diary. I was devastated and angry with Evan. We didn't talk that entire summer. He had simply vanished. It took years for me to forgive him for that. He did eventually approach me during our high school years, to try and explain himself, but I just wasn't going to have it. I was too hurt, too angry, and far too stubborn to let him.

Thank goodness for Leia, she really came through as a best friend. She's always been so up-beat and fun. She was actually elated that Evan was out of the picture—probably because she was afraid that if Evan and I ever became a couple, she and I would quickly lose contact.

I'm happy to report that when it finally did happen between Evan and me, Leia remained my very best friend and we still make lots of time for each other.

So much more happened before me and Evan finally got together. We'll get there soon enough.

Before starting high school, I had made a declaration that I was going to reinvent myself. Much to my mother's delight, I asked *her* to take me shopping for school clothes—not my father. I wanted to buy skirts and more feminine shoes. I needed a new image if I was going to be a new person.

She had all sorts of ideas and suggestions, but I hated all of them, of course. I wanted to look feminine, but not like I'd just rolled out of cheer camp. I wanted something more professional looking and dignified.

We bought a few skirts and about a hundred pairs of shoes. I've never really understood women's obsession with shoes, but my mother insisted and I didn't want to disappoint her. She had waited her entire life for that moment. Who was I to deprive her? Okay, I love shoes. Who doesn't?

When we started looking at tops and blouses, that's where my mother's excitement came to a screeching halt. I hated everything she suggested and refused to even try any of them on. I wanted shirts with long sleeves. I wanted flannels. I guess that was the Iowa girl in me—I still love a nice soft flannel, even with a skirt.

Our shopping day ended with me insisting on purchasing a couple of bow ties to wear with my flannels. I thought it was a cute look. I still wear them today, sometimes. I guess it's just my own personal touch.

If you could have only seen her face when I put one on. My poor mother.

Chapter 6

December 27, 2006

Dear Diary,

This year, the big Christmas block party was at Evan's house. And, this year, I lied about being sick so I wouldn't have to go.

My mother knew I was lying and tried to force me to come, but my dad talked her out of it and let me stay home. He knew why I didn't want to go. He's an awesome parent and a terrific human being. Thank you dad. You really are the best.

So, I wish I could tell you that not going to the party at Evan's house meant that I was successful in avoiding Evan the other night, but it didn't turn out at all as planned.

Mr. Milan, Evan's father, asked my wonderful mother where I was, right in front of Evan, and she told him that I wasn't feeling well and that I was still at home, all alone.

The genuinely nice and considerate Mr. Milan—perhaps Evan was adopted—had apparently told Evan that he should quickly make some soup and get his butt across the street and offer it to the sweet girl over there who was spending the big night of the party at home all by herself. UGH!

I was sitting on the couch in my peejays, hair a total mess, watching TV when Evan came a knockin' at my door.

I had absolutely no clue that it was him, so I just walked over and opened up.

YIKES!

There was Evan, with his stupid letterman jacket on—no letter, of course, FRESHMAN!—holding a Tupperware container filled with chicken noodle soup. He had a goofy smile on his face, but he still looked cuter than ever.

Forgive me. It was a moment of weakness. I'm not proud. But he did look good. I'm not gonna lie. Wouldn't it be lying to myself if I tried to deny that he looked good here? Not important—moving on.

NO, PENELOPE! I wasn't going to play that game. I hate Evan, remember? He and the worst best friend a person could ever have had betrayed me.

"What do you want, Evan?" was all I had to offer him. I refused to smile back. Sorry.

"My dad told me to bring you some soup to help you feel better. Do you think I could come in and talk?"

Adorable villain. That's what he was. He was simply adorable, but he was a villain all the same. I wasn't about to let him back into my heart, but he was too cute to turn away at the door. I let him in—to talk.

It's important to note something here, as a reminder to you—to myself. Why is Evan a villain? Not just because he went after my best friend. Sorry, former best friend. There's more to it than that. Evan allegedly didn't know I was head over heels for him—allegedly.

Scarlett knew, but this isn't about her. Had she come over to offer soup and ask to talk, the door would have been promptly slammed in her face. Excuse me, in both of her faces.

Evan is a villain because he, and also Scarlett, plus that idiot, Trevor, had reduced me to a weekend-and-summers-only friend once they got their in with the cool kids. I was good enough to come and hang out with, but only when no one else was around to see them spending time with that nerdy girl they were friends with as kids.

NOT COOL, EVAN. Not cool at all. And all the popularity in the world won't make that okay with me.

Good, we got that straight. That's important for what happened next.

Before he could say a word though, I asked him how Scarlett was. He needed to be reminded that I hated her. We would get to how I felt about him later—maybe. I hadn't made my mind up on that yet.

His answer shocked me a little bit and I lost my game face. "I wouldn't know, Pen. We broke up and she won't talk to me. I told her I wanted to stay friends, but she's pretty mad."

I ignored the fact that he called me Pen. I hate when he calls me Pen. I just nodded. "Hmmmm."

"How come we don't talk anymore, Pen?"

As if he didn't know. At least I thought he knew. How could he not know? He knows. He's not an idiot, and neither am I. I don't want to be the friend-on-the-weekend, or late at night, when no one's looking.

Game face back on.

I was flustered. I couldn't tell if I wanted to punch him for being so stupid, or kiss him for being so adorable. Maybe I should have kissed him and then punched him, and then sent him home to be as confused as I was.

I didn't do any of that I just sat there and didn't say a word.

"Anyway, I just wanted to make sure you were okay. I should get back to the party."

And that was that. I spent the night of the big party alone, unsure if I wanted to scream or if I wanted to cry. I do still hate Evan—don't I?

Oh, the drama. I remember that night like it was only a few Christmases ago. My poor, poor Evan. He tried so hard to be nice. And I just gave him the cold shoulder. It was true about him only wanting to be my friend when he had me alone. All the times at school, when he and Scarlett would see me, but pretend not to see me, really hurt, a lot.

We needed to have that conversation, but I was too afraid, or maybe too ashamed to have it. We would eventually talk about that, but much later on.

It wasn't easy for me to ignore Evan, but I was so angry at him. And at that time he didn't even know he had done anything wrong.

I hadn't told him directly how I felt about him. And if he knew that much, he hadn't figured out the whole weekend-only-friend thing that was happening. Honestly, how wise can a fourteen-year-old boy really be when it comes to matters of the heart?

He probably knew how I felt about him. After his relationship with Scarlett, if you could call it that, ended after just a few short months, some of his friends teased him that it was because he was secretly in love with me.

People in their circle who actually spoke with me had told me that Evan was harboring strong feelings for me. They claimed that those feelings had caused constant bickering between him and Scarlett. She would get so jealous and angry that the couple wasn't much fun to be around anymore.

I had no idea if what they were telling me was true or not, and I was far too stubborn back then to bother trying to find out. I probably should have reacted differently to Evan's olive branch that night. He was being sincere. We could have talked about how I felt about being his secret friend, but I was not having any of it. The pain was too fresh.

We obviously had a rekindling of our friendship, since we're about to get married, but it would take a little more time, and a little more suffering for that to happen.

I wonder how things would have played out if I had accepted Evan's offer then to start talking again. Would we have progressed to the same point where we are now? Would we have gotten here earlier in our lives?

There's another possibility to consider. Maybe the combative years that followed our time in high school helped to kindle a far more powerful fire between us that would have flamed out long ago had we acted on it too soon.

Oh, there's so much more to come.

Chapter 7

April 22, 2008

Dear Diary,

There's so much to talk about and I don't know where to start. I've been super busy, so please forgive me for neglecting you for so long.

What's happening? I thought you'd never ask. I started my first job a few weeks ago. I'm a cashier at Walmart. Don't laugh at me. It's not so bad. There's a ton of kids there and we make it fun.

So, one of those kids who makes it fun is Daniel Miller. He works in the checkout with me and he trained me to be a cashier. We go to school together, too, but he's never once tried to talk to me there.

That's not because he's like Evan and Scarlett—afraid to look uncool by lowering himself to speak with someone not in the *it crowd.* The reason for his silence at school was actually pretty infuriating to hear, but I decided not to be too angry about it.

My brother, Bradley, graduated last year and escaped to Ohio State—where he did not manage to walk onto the football team, not that I care, but he was pretty upset about that. Anyway, my dear older brother had spread the word LAST YEAR that any guy who tried to flirt with his baby sister would pay a dire price. I was strictly off limits and they shouldn't even attempt to talk to me.

Stupid, I know. When I called Bradley and asked him about it—correction, when I called him and yelled at him about it—he told me that I had made a huge leap, "in the looks department," from junior high to high school and guys were starting to notice me and talk.

Stupid? Yes we covered that—that's an incredibly stupid thing to say, but Bradley said it. He said all the, "Your sister's kinda hot now," talk was bothering him, a lot. After he said that, I lost track of why I was mad at him.

I never thought in a million years that guys would ever notice me, let alone talk about me in ways that would make my big brother blush.

So, back to the point. Poor Daniel, who has his driver's license, by the way, offered to drive me home from work sometime. When I eagerly took him up on that offer, we talked, and he said that he's been wanting to talk to me since last year, but he was petrified of Bradley.

After I told him that I would deal with my overly-protective brother, harshly, Daniel asked me out, like, on an actual date. Can you believe it? Well, I still can't believe it.

I said I'd love to, of course, and we made plans to go on our date—a date, where he would drive to my house, meet my parents, and then drive us to the movies, or dinner, or something. I have an actual date.

I said yes, but I have no idea if my parents are ever going to allow that to happen. Thank God Bradley is in Ohio, because he would NEVER allow that to happen. I'm going to work on getting dad's permission tomorrow and I'll get a yes out of him, even if I have to shed a tear or two. He'll cave. He always caves.

Dad can break the news to mom, but she'll probably do cartwheels at the thought of me putting down my book and going out with a friend. Still, I'd rather ask my dad if it's okay. He's actually willing to negotiate terms in such difficult situations. My mother may say no just because she can, and once she says no, there's never any yeses to follow.

No one will be breaking the news to Bradley—just saying.

I know you're thinking it, so I'll be the one to bring it up. What about Evan? Well, I'd be a liar if I said that Evan wasn't a factor in my decision to say yes to Daniel. I do still have feelings for him. I'll probably always have feelings for him.

Right now, those are feelings of anger and I'd like to get over them. Evan hasn't spoken to me since I don't even remember when. I don't think we've had one conversation since sophomore year started.

He's smiled at me once or twice in the halls. He's not in any of my classes, because he's not smart enough to be in any of my classes. It's not mean if it's true.

Actually—I have to be honest—he is definitely smart enough to be in all of my classes. But Evan has always been kind of an easy-way-out sort of person.

Speaking of easy, Evan has had four girlfriends since he and Scarlett broke up last year. FOUR! All cheerleaders. Are you shocked? No, me either.

Evan has clearly shown no interest in me, friend or more-than-friend, and it's absolutely not because he's afraid of my big brother.

It's time for me to move on and Daniel seems like the perfect person to move on with.

Daniel Miller was my first official boyfriend. He was such a nice kid—and very cute. He actually went to med school and became a doctor, like his father, I think. I'm really not sure what eventually became of him. He moved away from Pella after college and I haven't heard a peep since.

It took a lot of convincing, but my father did eventually allow me to go out on a date with Daniel. There was one condition though. He was required to come over and have dinner with us before my dad would agree to allow the date to proceed. Simply coming into the house on the night of our date and shaking dad's hand would not suffice. My father wanted to get to know the boy who was asking to take his only daughter out on her first date.

Daniel was a good sport and agreed to the terms. When he eventually came over for dinner, he blew my parents away. He had my mom at, "My dad's a doctor," but my dad wasn't such an easy nut to crack.

My father tried to play hardball, but then he took one look at the stern gesture on my face and his plan was foiled. I didn't even have to shed a tear.

He proceeded to give Daniel the typical grilling expected from a father speaking to a boy who wanted to date his daughter, but it was pretty obvious that the answer would be yes.

The two *men* had very little in common. Daniel was a bookworm, like me, and my father is much more like Evan. My dad hated that Daniel was a soccer player. "Ever consider trying out for the football team?"

At least he played a sport, so he earned about a half of a point in that category—by my father's point scale.

Aside from the fond memories of Daniel, this entry made me smile because it reminded me of how loving and protective Bradley was—and still is. He's literally my father in younger form. He's my dad's mini me.

Bradley and I are very close. When Evan and I are married, I can see us spending a lot of time with Bradley and his wife. The four of us are already good friends. Hopefully we can continue the same types of traditions and shared family gathering that my family and Evan's family had enjoyed for as long as I can remember.

Of course, Evan and I had a long way to go from the time of this entry. During sophomore year in high school, Evan and I were probably the furthest from friends that we had ever been. We almost never spoke, and that continued for a few years.

We kept in contact, mostly by chance meetings at school or the very few family gatherings that Evan actually made an appearance at.

I think my rejecting his peace offering during his family's Christmas party the year before had actually hurt him. Looking back at the diary entries, I'm actually kind of proud of the maturity I showed at such a young age.

We both had a lot to learn. I know that even during our high-school separation, we both had feelings for each other. It was obvious. Our friends saw it and constantly reminded us of it. Everyone told us we were meant for each other, even then.

It must have been written somewhere in the town by-laws, "Evan and Penelope shall one day be married." There was no way either of us would have agreed to that in the spring of 2008.

Chapter 8

November 28, 2008

Dear Diary,

We had a really nice Thanksgiving yesterday. Grammy came over and helped my helpless mother create the best Thanksgiving meal we've ever had. It was a great day for sure.

It was a great day, that is, until it wasn't a great day. It was great until Evan's family showed up later in the day for desserts and drinks, like they do for every Thanksgiving.

Why was that so terrible? Do I even have to tell you who ruined it for me?

Let's go back to some things that happened before Thanksgiving. Evan, with the help of his father, has started a landscaping business. If I weren't so mad at him right now, I would actually be pretty proud of him. He's doing really well. He's got customers all over Pella. He's even got a few trucks and plows for snow removal this winter.

So, what's the problem? Well, the talk around school is that Evan offered a job to Scarlett. Now, I'm not so petty that I can't deal with the fact that Scarlett will be working for Evan during the summer. That's not the problem. The problem is what she's being hired to do for Evan and his pig-employees.

You see, Scarlett doesn't know a thing about landscaping. She's never even mowed her own lawn. Why would she be hired by a landscaping company if she has no idea how to handle a mower, or a rake, or any other gardening tool?

It seems Evan has asked Scarlett to join his landscaping crew this summer to not work at all. Scarlett has been hired to show up in a bikini and sunbathe while Evan and his friends do the actual landscaping work.

DISGUSTING!

You know Evan and I haven't been talking for a while now, but I thought I knew him better than that. This is not something the Evan who I've known my entire life would ever dream of doing. This is the new, not-so-improved Evan. This is some guy I don't even know at all. This is a guy I don't even want to know.

So when he came over with his family, I completely ignored him. I tried to not even look at him. I tried, but I may have given him a glance or two. It's been a long time since we've been in the same room. He's still Evan, after all.

He asked me to go outside and talk a few times and I pretended that I didn't hear him. He asked a lot of times, actually, and I felt bad about ignoring him. And then, I thought about Scarlett lying there in her bikini while his friends drooled over her. And then, I stopped feeling bad about it.

HOW COULD HE DO THAT?

It seems I've been crushing on the wrong guy for my entire life. I don't know if I'll ever respect him after this one. How can I?

The sad part is, I've dated a couple of so-called nice guys and I couldn't stand to be around them either. Leia says it's because, for some crazy reason, I'm STILL hung up on Evan.

Daniel was just about perfect. Cute, funny, smart, and my parents loved him. My mom would have maybe even left my dad for him. At least that's the impression I got.

That only lasted three months before I couldn't stand the sound of his voice anymore.

He would call, EVERY NIGHT, and be like, "Hi, babe, it's Daniel. What are you doing right now?"

"Gee, Daniel. Err, I mean, *babe.* It's nine o'clock at night and I'm in my room alone. What do you think I'm doing? What am I always doing when you call, every day, at the exact same time? I'm reading. I'm always reading. And this book is far more interesting than hearing you talk like a baby over the phone."

Poor Daniel. He probably deserved better than me and my little attitude. I just couldn't stand it anymore.

Fact is, I'm a junior in high school and there isn't a single guy in my school that I am even a little bit interested in right now. This annoying little fact wouldn't be so bad if this was senior year. At least then, college would be a lot sooner. New, smarter people. Mature men, not boys.

Ugh. All of that's still a year and a half away.

I was so cold to Evan that Thanksgiving night. If his entire family weren't at my house, I'm sure he would have left the party and never spoken to me again. I'm surprised he didn't just do that anyway. Maybe he didn't want to explain to his parents that he and I weren't even friends anymore.

That Scarlett in a bikini thing was all over school and I was shocked that he would ever even suggest doing something like that. It went beyond just showing off his new business in front of his friends. I was so unbelievably disappointed in him when I had heard about that.

Evan's landscaping business, which he still has today, really hit the ground running. It didn't hurt that his family name was on the trucks, and his father bankrolled the entire thing—at least in the beginning.

Everyone knew Evan's family name. His father was a football star. His older brother, Thomas, was a football star. Evan was a football star. The entire town had gotten used to worshiping and cheering for a Milan for years.

Evan's father also owned, and still owns, a very successful business right here in Pella that manufactures and distributes golf accessories.

It was Mr. Milan's dream that one of his two sons would take the reins from him after he retired, but that doesn't seem to be a possibility now.

The business could actually remain in the Milan family when Mr. Milan retires, but we have a lot to talk about before we get there.

The elder of Mr. Milan's sons, Thomas, has a great job at Pella Windows and Doors that he started right after college. He never had any interest in the golf accessory business—or in working for his dad.

Evan is doing great things with his landscaping business. And though Mr. Milan wanted at least one of his son's to work for him one day, it's not surprising that he encouraged Evan to go off and start his own company.

After all, that's exactly what Mr. Milan did when he was a little older than Evan and he got his start as an entrepreneur. And I'm sure he thoroughly enjoyed watching Evan make a go of it. Mr. Milan is a very nice man and an excellent father.

Sons of Pella fathers tend to follow in their daddy's footsteps, in one way or another. That's exactly what Daniel Miller had done when he became a doctor, though he did eventually leave Pella.

Daniel, my first boyfriend, really was perfect back then. He's probably still perfect now, but it just wasn't written in the stars for Daniel and me.

Daniel did this thing with his voice when we talked on the phone and it drove me positively batty—and not in a good way. He constantly spoke in baby talk and I hated it. Or maybe I just didn't like him enough to tell him that I really wished he would speak normally during our phone conversations. And maybe I should have done that before I snapped at him and dumped him.

Daniel was the first in a not-so-long line of very short high school romances for me. I found something I couldn't stand about every boy and ended each doomed relationship abruptly—and typically in cruel fashion.

None of them were smart enough, or tall enough, or they were too shy in front of my parents, or they weren't shy enough in front of my parents. I hated the way they talked, or the way they breathed with their mouth open—you get the picture.

The simple truth was clear, but I couldn't see it at the time. I didn't want to see it at the time. None of them were ever Evan enough.

Chapter 9

August 8, 2010

Dear Diary,

I got my new college roomie's contact information—finally. Her name is Tara Benton and she's from Indiana. I really hope she's easygoing and nice, because, as I'll explain in a minute, I suck at making new friends—apparently.

I read Tara's profile and we seem to share a lot of common interests. I'm super excited for college. Well, at least I was. After what happened earlier tonight, I can barely think about that.

I'm not moving to Grinnell for a couple of weeks, but I plan on calling Tara and getting to know her a little bit before that. Hopefully, we can coordinate what we'll each be bringing to our room. Maybe we can share some things and each have less to pack. Yes, that was absolutely my dad's idea, but I like it.

So, what would you guess has me so distracted? I've been waiting for this moment for years. You'd think I'd be bouncing off the walls right now.

Is it Evan? BINGO! Great guess.

He kept calling me, over and over, leaving messages that we absolutely need to talk before we both leave for school. I tried to just ignore him.

He's going to Iowa State—that's a huge shock, I know. Everyone from Pella goes to Iowa State. Anyway, Iowa State is an hour away from Grinnell College, so it's not like one of us is moving to China. If he needs to reach me so badly, he can, even after we head to school.

However, Evan refused to take no answer for an answer and came over last night—uninvited. My positively clueless mother let him in. Thanks mom.

I didn't want to see him before heading off to school. I didn't need the distraction.

I had moved on from the ghost formerly known as Evan Milan. Before tonight, I don't remember the last time we had a conversation with more words than, "Hey, how's it going?" followed by, "Good, you?"

So, my mom walked him to my room, and knocked on the door. "Penelope, sweetheart, there's someone here to visit with you."

I just assumed it was Leia and replied, "Mom, why didn't you just tell her to come up?"

"It's Evan."

Total and utter panic ensued. Picture me, in my pajamas, scrambling all over my room, trying to get my clothes up off the floor, wondering how horrible my hair was, and about to kill my mother. Got it? Yeah, that's what it looked like.

"I'll be right out. Don't come in!" I yelled back.

There was no way he was coming into my room.

I got dressed, made myself presentable, and found Evan waiting for me in the living room with my mom—watching TV. My mom had this really dumb smile from ear to ear.

Oh, I'll deal with you later, lady, I thought to myself.

I just smiled at them both and tried to keep my cool. "Can we go outside?" I asked Evan.

I was furious, but curious. It had been so long since Evan came over for one of our little talks. Months? Years? Maybe years. He knew I didn't like him very much. I made it pretty obvious at school. Why was he here?

"Pen, I've been wanting to talk to you for like, forever. I hate the way things are with us. Can we just talk for one night, like we used to?"

"It's been a while, Evan. What's on your mind?" I answered with as little expression on my face as I could possibly display.

"What happened with us? Why do you hate me so much?"

I wanted to kill him. Was he really asking me that question?

"Oh, Evan. This goes way back to junior high, and all the way through high school. Remember when you and Scarlett used to be my best friends?"

"Yeah, I do. But what the heck happened?"

"Well, for starters, once you two got popular you left me in the dust. I guess I wasn't cool enough to be around anymore?"

"We still made time for you. We did all kinds of stuff together."

"Only at home. Never at school. And *never* when your cool friends were around."

I could feel my face turning red, but I kept going. "This is ridiculous. I can't even believe we're having this conversation right now."

And then Evan handed me some truth. Well, his truth. I'm still wondering if I should take what he said seriously, or if he was just trying to make me feel bad.

Am I partially to blame? Mostly to blame? Ugh. I might share at least some of the blame, but I'm doing my best to think of something else. LIKE COLLEGE!

"We tried to include you—a lot." he claimed. "I guess we could have tried harder and I'm really sorry about that. That's on me. But you know how you are around new people. You get all judgy and act super shy. You basically ignored our new friends and it made everyone uncomfortable. You suck at making new friends, Pen. You know this."

"Whatever, Evan. And then you and Scarlett start dating behind my back? What's up with that?"

"God, that was so long ago. I wanted to tell you, but she begged me not to. She said she would talk with you about it later."

"Well, I guess she never did. I mean, why bother, right?"

Evan saw that I was getting upset and he quickly softened his tone. I wanted to go back into my house and slam the door in his face, but I needed to bring up one more thing—the Scarlett-in-a-bikini-at-work thing.

"That never happened. She asked me if she could come to work with us in the summers, and then Trevor brought up all of that stupid bikini stuff. I never said any of that. I'd lose all of my customers if I tried to pull something like that. Pen, you know I would never do something like that. Think about it. My business is really important to me."

Trevor. Of course it was Trevor. But does it matter? Evan didn't exactly do anything to quell the rumors that spread afterward.

Trevor is still an idiot, by the way. Just wanted to make that clear.

It turns out that Scarlett helps Evan with keeping his records and bills straight. She's actually handling most of his accounting stuff. Apparently she's pretty good at it. Who knew she had a brain? I sure didn't.

All the kids at school just took the Trevor rumor and ran with it. And I was so mad about what I had heard that I never bothered to find out the truth.

Okay, so that part is definitely my fault.

If I think about all of it now, sometimes I wonder if Evan really has no clue why I've been so cold to him through most of high school. If that's true, why is he still willing to talk to me? What the heck is on that boy's mind?

So, I'm trying not to think about all of it. Does any of this matter now anyway? We're going to college—two different colleges.

I didn't know what else to say to Evan, and I guess he didn't know what to say to me.

"Well, I'm glad we had this talk, Pen. I'm headed back to Ames tomorrow. Trevor, a couple of other guys, and I got an off-campus apartment. We already moved in on August first."

"Wow, that's pretty cool." My mind was racing. I was still speechless.

"Do you think we can try to keep in touch?"

"I guess. I don't see why not." After what he told me, how could I say no?

Evan went home and I went back to my room to write all of this to you.

So, here I am. I'm totally confused and thinking about a million things and not the one thing I thought I couldn't wait another day for—finally going to college.

I wish I could say that this conversation with Evan turned things around quickly for us, but it didn't. We each went off to college and it was months before we spoke again.

Evan was in his glory at Iowa State. He and his friends had the time of their lives—as anyone who knew them would have expected.

I didn't really enjoy college like I had imagined I would. I didn't gel with my roommate or anyone else, besides maybe a couple of professors. But those weren't the relationships I had hoped to forge.

Yes, the people were more mature—well, slightly more mature. And despite the confusion I had experienced from the night described in my diary entry, I got to put all my troubles about my friendship with Evan behind me for a while.

Evan and I did become friends again, but there was distance. We obviously didn't talk much or see each other often. We made an effort to spend time together, but for the first few semesters of college we only saw each other during the summer months and winter breaks. Still, we were building on our friendship.

Tara, my roommate, was really nice and we got along fine, but we weren't the best of friends. She quickly developed lots of friendships with other students and I didn't take advantage of those opportunities when they had presented themselves.

Maybe Evan was right. Of course he was right—I sucked at making new friends.

I had one true friend at Grinnell—my Aunt Laura. She's my father's sister and an Environmental Studies professor at Grinnell College.

Aunt Laura almost never came to visit us in Pella, and we never went to see her at Grinnell. I had met her a few times, at various formal family gatherings—weddings and/or funerals. She and my mother have never gotten along.

Aunt Laura, and just about everyone else at Grinnell, is extremely political. Grinnell is one of the most liberal colleges in America. Let's just say my mother and Aunt Laura have opposing views on most things and leave it at that.

Aside from being on the opposite side of the political spectrum from my mother, Aunt Laura lives an *alternate lifestyle*. That's my mom's way of saying that Aunt Laura is a lesbian. She thinks it's polite to phrase it that way—I don't agree, and neither does Aunt Laura.

I didn't go to Grinnell for politics. I don't consider myself to be a very political person. Grinnell College is perhaps one of the most prestigious schools in Iowa. It's quite difficult to get into, and I got in. So I went, and I'm happy that I did—even if things didn't play out socially like I had hoped they would.

I did develop a great relationship with my aunt while attending Grinnell. She talked me through some complicated times. I'm so happy that I got to know her as well as I have. She's still a source of terrific advice for me.

As you'd expect, most of those complicated times had a lot to do with my difficulties making friends. And, of course, with my difficulties understanding my feelings for Evan.

Chapter 10

February 13, 2012

Dear Diary,

I just *hugged* Evan goodbye yesterday morning after he finally came out to Grinnell to visit me and stayed the night in my room. No, nothing happened. No, I didn't want anything to happen.

Maybe I wanted *something* to happen, but nothing happened.

Evan has a girlfriend. And even though he told me that he would dump her when he got back to Ames if I told him to, that is NOT my style. If he wanted to get something started between us, he should have dumped her before he came to see me, right?

Asking me if I wanted him to dump his girlfriend just annoyed me and killed the mood—

not that there really was a mood to kill. I'm not going to do something like that to some innocent girl who I've never met before—even if she's probably not so innocent. She's probably just like Scarlett and all of the other girls Evan's ever dated.

I'm still glad that he came for a visit. I'm just not glad that I'm stuck here, alone, wondering about what's happening, or not happening, between us.

He was so free and playful the whole time he was here. It was like we were little kids again and there wasn't any drama about Scarlett, girlfriends, or whether we should be friends or more than friends. We just goofed off and enjoyed each other's company.

It was a really nice visit—right up until he said he had to go and then we had that super awkward hug. That's when it all came back in a giant wave of weirdness that still has me feeling utterly confused about EVERYTHING.

Tara went and stayed with a friend so Evan and I could have some privacy. I felt a little weird about having a guy over and sending her to stay the night with a friend—even though it was her idea. She just made me promise that if anything were to happen, it would happen in my bed, not hers.

What actually happened was I slept in her bed and Evan slept in mine. Well, I didn't actually sleep at all. I just stared at the ceiling all night and wondered if ANYTHING was going to happen. Nothing happened. Nothing but listening to the awful sound of Evan snoring all night. I guess his mind wasn't racing all over the place like mine was.

FIGURES.

Evan and I had such a terrific time together. We took a tour of campus, where he laughed and made fun of all the "hippies" and "tree huggers," but that didn't bother me too much. He wasn't completely wrong, except for the name calling. We have a really, really liberal group of people here. I happen to love the mix of ideas and expressions. Apparently, Evan wasn't impressed.

He told me he signed up to play club lacrosse next month. Of course he's playing lacrosse—I'll refrain from name calling of my own. Anyway, he brought a couple lacrosse sticks and a ball and we played catch in MacEachron Field, in the middle of all the dorms. Well, he played catch and I played chase-after-the-ball when I failed to catch it—over and over.

I took him to Pagliai's for pizza. You can't come to Grinnell and not go to Pagliai's. Not doing that would be a huge fail. It would be like going to Pella and not visiting The Vermeer Windmill. You just don't do that.

After dinner we went to my room and talked for hours, until Evan fell asleep and I laid awake in Tara's bed all night.

He got up a little early, woke me up—well, he shook me while I pretended to sleep and then I pretended to wake up—and then said he had to get going.

That's when we had that horribly awkward hug.

I spent the rest of Sunday with Aunt Laura, laying on her couch while she graded papers, or tests. I don't remember which. I was barely conscious.

Oh, my gosh. I nearly forgot the most interesting part of the weekend. Evan invited me to go to Daytona next month with him, his friends, and probably his girlfriend, for spring break.

I told him I'd think about it and get back to him. I don't need to think about it. I don't want to go. It's just not my thing. Just like every *Thirsty Thursday* when Tara asks me if I want to go to some frat party and get drunk—that's just not my thing either.

I told Aunt Laura that I didn't want to go and she said I should. "You need to start saying yes to some of these invites. You're a college kid. You should be having fun with other college kids."

"But I have fun with you, Aunt Laura."

"Very funny. You're welcome here anytime you want to come, but when your mother complains that you spend too much time with me, make sure you tell her that I'm doing my best to push you out to spend more time with kids your own age. That woman actually thinks I'm trying to convert you into living an *alternate lifestyle*, like me."

"Wait, you mean turn me into a lesbian? Oh my goodness. Could you actually do that for me, please? It would make my life far less complicated."

"Not funny, Penelope. Not funny at all."

Who's laughing?

This was sophomore year at Grinnell College. Evan and I had made a promise over winter break that one of us would go and visit the other at school that semester. So, he came to see me.

I hadn't remembered how close we actually came to getting involved back then, until I read the entry above. I remember the visit and the flirting, but I forgot long ago that he came out and asked me if I wanted him to break up with his girlfriend. Why didn't I say yes? Oh, yes, that's right. I was being moral. Silly me.

When I think about those moments today, I'm surprised that Evan didn't just give up. He kept trying to tell me how he felt for years, and I kept rejecting him.

Part of me is proud of my younger self for sticking to my principles, but if I knew then what I know today, that night would have gone quite differently.

Tara was so disappointed in me when I told her that nothing had happened. She was shocked when she finally met Evan. She kept telling me she couldn't believe how hot he was.

"Oh my God, Penelope. Why haven't you locked that down?"

She was so excited for me and immediately offered to find another place to stay while Evan was at Grinnell.

After he went back to Ames, she joked that I was insane to let him leave without attacking him while I had the perfect chance. She said she may as well have slept in her own bed that night—maybe she could have done something about it herself.

That was my last semester with Tara as my roommate. She paired up with a friend the next year and I ended up moving into a single and becoming a Resident Advisor. We hardly spoke for the next two years and I haven't seen her at all since college.

My Aunt Laura was right to try and convince me to accept invitations from kids my own age—even if they were doing things that I just wasn't really into at the time.

I didn't have to partake in the partying or drinking. No one actually expected me to. They were just trying to be my friend. I spent way too much time alone at school, or over at my Aunt Laura's place.

I was used to spending time alone through all my four years of high school. I had my father and I had my books, and I guess that was enough—but it wasn't really enough. I guess those lonely habits just continued into college.

By my junior year, those invitations became few and far between.

Chapter 11

May 31, 2014

Dear Diary,

I have a job. Correction, I have a fabulous job. I never thought I'd be in the golf accessories biz, but that's where I've landed. Mr. Milan—that's Evan's dad—reached out to me three days before graduation and asked if I'd come to the plant in Pella to have a conversation with him and his Operations Manager, who happens to be retiring soon.

I said, "Sure, why not. I could use some interview practice. Thank you Mr. Milan." I had no idea they were actually serious about offering me a job. I felt pretty silly about how I answered him when I realized they were. Oops.

Mr. Milan's golf accessories business is pretty huge in Pella. He's no Pella Windows and Doors, but he still has it going on in town. He's well-loved and very well respected. The guy could literally run for Mayor if he chose to.

I'm honestly not sure why he reached out to me. He has two sons who are both college graduates, and Evan has a business degree from Iowa State.

I'm sure everyone, including Mr. Milan, expected Evan to go to work for his father after college—especially after Thomas went to another company a couple years ago. Thomas got hooked up pretty nicely at Pella Windows and Doors. He's doing really well.

One thing's for sure, my getting this job is going to help calm my dad down. He was so mad when I told him I didn't want to go for my Master's.

"I think I've just had enough of college," was not the answer he wanted to hear when he asked me why I was stopping with just a Bachelor's. But now that I have a great job, he can chill out—at least a little bit.

So, Mr. Milan didn't want to give me the job title of Operations Manager—at least not right away. He told me that I would have to earn the title if I wanted it. Dude, I want it.

The guy doing that job now plans to stick around just long enough to personally train me and make sure it's an easy transition from him to me before he retires. So, he's got one foot out the door already. Unless I completely screw it up, the title is mine.

Right now I'm the Assistant Operations Manager. How fancy. I'm pretty psyched about it. My focus will be to remove the word *assistant* as quickly as possible.

Thank goodness for the paycheck because I'm swimming in Grinnell College-generated debt right now. I don't know if I could have even afforded a Master's Degree. Well, I suppose I could have, but I'm pretty sure if I went that route I'd be paying off student loans until age fifty.

I just had to go to a private college and not Iowa State like everyone else from Pella. It's the cost of daring to be different I suppose. I like to think it was worth it, but something tells me that

Mr. Milan would have offered me the job no matter where I went to school.

Anyway, back to the job. I'm gonna need to talk this over with Evan. Does he plan to mow grass and shovel snow for the rest of his life? I have no idea why this job is my job and not his. Maybe Mr. Milan offered him something better?

Wait a minute. What if Evan is actually going to be in a position higher than me? Is there any way in hell that I could survive with Evan as my boss?

I need to call that boy tonight and find out if he's going to work for his father. Maybe I should have done that before I accepted the offer.

I called Evan minutes after I finished this diary entry. I knew he was doing well with his landscaping business, but I never believed he would continue with that after he graduated from college—I don't think anyone did, especially Mr. Milan.

I expected Evan to tell me he had accepted some high-level management position at the company and I'd be reporting to him. Instead, he shocked me and told me his father had offered him a job and he respectfully turned him down.

Evan congratulated me and said I would be in very good hands at a very good company. I found out later that the job that Evan had turned down was the same job that I had just accepted, which was an incredible honor for me.

I replied to Evan that I was touched that his father thought so highly of me, and after a long pause, Evan told me that Mr. Milan wasn't the only one. After that, the conversation died and we said our awkward goodbyes.

Mr. Milan's dream of eventually passing his company's operation over to one or both of his sons was on hold, at least for the time being. Did he somehow know at the time that making me his Operations Manager and then spending several years molding me into his protégé would keep the company in the family? The world may never know—I'm just getting started. Though I've considered it, I'm not about to ask him that question now. Not appropriate.

I remember leaving Grinnell College and moving back to Pella. I was home for a short time, but quickly found an apartment of my own downtown. My dad cried after moving me in and assembling all of my furniture piece by piece.

"This is where the Powerful Penelope Pym gets started."

I felt like a conquering hero, but I may have shed a tear or two when I saw my dad cry.

The night before I left Grinnell, my Aunt Laura took me out to dinner to celebrate and say goodbye.

I still make time to visit with her as often as I can. We formed a pretty strong bond during my college years and our friendship is as strong now as it was back then.

Aunt Laura had some special news to share with me at our celebratory dinner. She introduced me to her new partner, Ella. Ella is also a professor at Grinnell College, but I hadn't met her before that night.

They were great together, and I was so happy for Aunt Laura. She definitely found her match. Such a terrific person deserved all the happiness the world had to offer.

When we got our drinks, I raised my glass to toast their new relationship. "To finding love and happiness."

We all sipped our drinks and before we set our glasses down, Aunt Laura raised hers up again. She waited for Ella and me to raise ours up with hers and gave a mischievous grin.

"To my lovely niece. May you and Evan finally stop tiptoeing around the obvious and declare your love for each other. It's about time for the two of you to find the love and happiness that's been right in front of you for years."

Oh, Aunt Laura.

Chapter 12

June 19, 2014

Dear Diary,

It's Thursday afternoon and everyone from work is somewhere downtown having a drink, like they always do on Thursdays, to blow off steam and just enjoy each other's company outside of the office. I'm at home, alone, writing to you.

It's my own fault that I'm not out having fun with my coworkers. Several of them had reached out to ask if I was going. People mentioned the tradition to me lots of times in the few weeks I've been there. I just keep making up lame excuses about why I can't go this time, but maybe I'll go next time.

Well, I'm sure that eventually they'll stop asking or even mentioning it to me at all. But when or if that ever happens, I bet if I were to ask someone about it, they'd tell me where they're going and I could join them. I'm just not sure if I'll ever want to do that.

I wish I wanted to—I bet it would make things a lot more fun at work. I just don't—at least not right now.

I'm told that Mr. Milan hardly ever goes. He said he wants to let them have their fun. He doesn't want anyone to be worried about having the boss around—but they adore him and I'm sure him being there would only make everyone adore him even more.

I'm pretty sure that most people at work don't adore me, and that's fine. I haven't been super social there so far. I'm there to learn as much as possible from Larry—that's the current Operations Manager's name—before he retires and I take over. I'm focusing on that right now and nothing else matters.

Larry likes me, thank goodness. He says I'm a human sponge, capable of learning and absorbing more information than anyone he's ever seen before. He told Mr. Milan that I'm ready to take over *now.* And then he reassured both Mr. Milan and me that he meant it by setting his official retirement date. He'll be gone on the week before the Fourth of July.

Larry told me today that I need to lighten up and join him and the rest of the crew for a beer after work.

No means no Larry.

So, yeah, a sixty-two-year-old man is apparently more fun, per his peers, than me. I'm the fuddy duddy. He's the cool one. That's just awesome. I wish I cared more about that, but I don't.

I'm going to pass on drinks with the crew, again, but I'm wondering if passing is the right idea. Maybe I should try to be more social at work. Maybe I should try to be more social in general.

No, I don't want to go—honestly.

On another awkward note, Evan comes by the office just about every dang day to have lunch with his father. It's actually really nice and it makes him even more adorable than he obviously already is. I hate it and love it at the same time. Is that even possible? I think it is.

Last week Scarlett came with him and sucked every last bit the adorableness out of the building.

Apparently she's gone and got herself a fiancé, and it's not Evan

HALLELUJAH!

She didn't come out and tell me, we still aren't exactly on speaking terms.

She did smile and wave to me when she came to the office. I'm not sure, but I may have waved back. I honestly don't remember.

She has an engagement ring on her finger. How nice for her.

Mr. Milan says that Scarlett and Evan are doing an outstanding job running Evan's business together. He compliments her quite often and then gives me a mischievous grin just about every time.

I think he wants me to react in some way, but I'm never going to take the bait. Nice try buddy. I don't think that I give that man enough credit. He definitely does pay attention.

Back to Evan. Every time that beautiful man comes to see his father, he stops by my office and we talk about what's going on in our lives. So far he's failed to mention his latest new girlfriend, who he's been dating for a couple weeks. I got that little nugget from his father.

Oh, and for the record, Mr. Milan doesn't really like the new girlfriend so much. He says, and I'll quote, "She's by far the most useless human being my oblivious son has ever become involved with."

When he said that to me, I couldn't help but let out a quick laugh that I tried to cover up with a cough. Mr. Milan wasn't fooled.

"One of these days that boy will grow up and come to his senses. One day, he'll even find the right girl. That is, if he hasn't already."

Gee, Mr. Milan. Whatever do you mean?

I wish I could list all of the things that working for Mr. Milan has taught me over the years. Maybe, someday, that might become an entire book of its own. He's truly a second father to me and I love him dearly.

The early days in the office were a little tough for me. It wasn't the job, so much. I feel like I really came into my own as an Operations Manager—Assistant Operations Manager.

The work part came pretty naturally and easy for me. It was the whole office dynamic and social culture that thing I struggled with—tremendously.

Mr. Milan runs his business like a family. There's a tight-knit environment among the employees and management takes pride in that and does a lot to cultivate it. I know lots of small businesses say the same thing about their company culture, but it really exists within our walls.

Insert a young Penelope Pym into that ecosystem. She's exceedingly shy, she's been described, fairly, as tremendously antisocial, and she's got a chip on her shoulder the size of Texas.

I wish that was all, but there's more. It seems pretty obvious to everyone that she's got something to prove to the world. She also believes she's about ten times smarter than anyone else in the building. What could possibly go wrong?

Yeah, it started a little rough for me but it was my own doing. I'm so very happy to tell you that it got better.

When I look back at this entry, I feel like these were the early stages of Evan and me finally coming together toward something meaningful—though it still took a while to get where we are today. I remember being touched by his relationship with his father—a man I completely adored and respected.

I know that I'd always expressed plenty of infatuation with Evan, but at the time of this entry, I was really starting to develop stronger feelings toward him. When I witnessed how he and his dad truly loved and appreciated each other, my infatuation became something more.

But, like most of the times I had begun to hope for more with Evan, he had some fragile relationship going on with someone else.

He had told me multiple times that he would break off whatever meaningless relationship he was in if I would just tell him to.

I hated when he did that. It was as if he wanted me to end his relationship with someone he didn't care about for him. I refused to be used in that way—even by Evan. Especially by Evan.

During the rare times when he was single—or when I believed that he might be single—I just never had the nerve to express how I felt. Or maybe I was petrified of rejection in favor of someone I wasn't told about who I somehow believed was inferior to me in every way. I know that's wildly inappropriate, but that was how I felt, maybe.

Chapter 13

June 7, 2015

Dear Diary,

I'm sitting here on a Sunday night wondering if I should even bother going into the office tomorrow. I'm angry about work and utterly confused about Evan—as I have been my entire life.

I realize the topics of work and Evan aren't totally related, but he'll be around at least a few times during the week to visit with his father for lunch. He'll pop in to visit with me, like he always does, and I don't know if I want to see him right now.

Why all the anger and confusion, you ask?

Well, let's start with the work issue. We're going on about one full year of existing without an Operations Manager at my place of employment. I mean, we have an actual Operations Manager—that's me—but my title is still Assistant Operations Manager.

How can that be? Who are you the assistant to?

Right? How can I be an assistant to a person who retired a year ago? Also, before Larry left, he told Mr. Milan that I was the right person for the job and that I would be great at it. He felt very comfortable riding off into the sunset to enjoy his retirement. And I haven't bothered him once for help on anything since he left.

Despite all of that, I'm still the Assistant Operations Manager and I don't know what I've done wrong. I work hard. I do a great job. Mr. Milan has told me that several times.

So why no promotion? Why am I doing the job I was hired to do, but not receiving the recognition that I should be getting?

I think it's time for me and my boss to have a chat and we'll do that tomorrow.

And yes, I'm kind of freaking out about the whole thing, perhaps more so than I should be. I love Mr. Milan, don't get me wrong. And I really don't want to quit my job—I actually like my job. I'm really good at my job. I mentioned that, right?

So that's on my mind, along with something that happened at work a couple of days ago—on Friday. Let's discuss the Evan portion of my Sunday-night woes.

Oh—fair warning—this one is a doozy.

Evan came to my office before going to lunch with his father and something happened that pretty much changes everything.

He's flirted with me a thousand times, and I've done the same with him. We never take it too far and neither of us has ever taken it too seriously. And then this happened.

Evan came right out and asked, "Why haven't you and I ever dated?"

I thought he was kidding and I came back with something snarky. "I don't know, have you looked in the mirror lately? You know that you're not as pretty as you once were, right?"

"I'm being serious, Pen. You and I are basically perfect for each other. Why do we keep on avoiding it?"

WHAT? Where did that come from?

Brian D. Campbell

I was speechless. I mean, I wanted to tell him that I've been in love with him since kindergarten, but he was always either too cool for me, or too mixed up with some cheerleader, or dating my best friend.

"Aren't you gonna say something?"

"I don't know. Maybe you should ask your girlfriend the same question and see what she thinks."

INSTANT REGRET—but it had to be said. Didn't it?

There was a long, awkward pause and I waited for him to tell me he'd dump her if I wanted him to—so I could get up and punch him in his beautiful face—but he didn't.

So then, instead of replying with something completely Evan-like, as I was totally expecting him to do, he just pursed his lips, looked at the floor, and shook his head up and down.

"I don't know what to say, Evan. You have a girlfriend and I'm not about to say or do anything that might undermine your relationship."

In other words, you beautiful jackass, make up your damn mind about who you want. Then, come back and see me so we can have this conversation when you're actually single for once. I'll be here and I'll be all ears.

Evan said nothing. He just turned around and started to walk out of my office.

He stopped when he reached the door and turned around. And then he dropped this bomb on my world, "I broke up with Angela three days ago. She kept insisting that I'm in love with someone else and it was driving both of us crazy."

I had no response. I've been waiting for this moment for basically my entire life and I froze.

"Turns out she might be right."

He hit me with that, and then he walked away.

To say that I was stunned by Evan coming out and telling me that he thought he was in love with me would be an understatement. I was in shock.

I should have seized on the opportunity the moment it presented itself. Evan had finally broken up with one of his many girlfriends, not because I told him to, but because he wanted to—because he had finally chosen me. And I sat there, like a lump, with nothing to say.

I let him walk away without any effort to stop him. I had no idea at the time how difficult it was for him to say those things. I also had no idea how long it would be before we would continue the conversation that he was so brave to start. We both desperately wanted things to finally play out for us, but we were afraid to talk about it.

Why were we so afraid? Maybe it was the fear of losing a lifelong friend. Maybe it was the thought of leaving such a wonderful comfort zone that we had both built around each other.

Let's just say we didn't continue that conversation right away—I wish I had a logical explanation for that. The good news, as we already know per all of my spoilers, is that things did eventually play out. We did eventually end up together—eventually. And it didn't cost us our friendship.

The rest of this entry was about Mr. Milan taking his time to promote me to Operations Manager. He had his reasons, but, of course, I was too young and inexperienced to understand them at the time.

Though it was a great source of agitation for me, it did eventually get resolved. I marched straight to his office on that Monday morning, like I said I would, and we had a conversation.

I have to admit that the talk didn't go as I had planned it would. I can't say that I enjoyed *that conversation* very much. But things at work eventually played out to a happy conclusion as well.

Mr. Milan is a very wise and tactical person. What he proposed was nothing short of genius and it helped me make an extremely important change of course in the way I handled myself at work—and even in life.

Chapter 14

July 24, 2015

Dear Diary,

I had literally the best day ever at work today. Mr. Milan saw fit to FINALLY promote me to Operations Manager. He also gave me a much larger raise than I was expecting—which was nice, very nice.

Let me tell you, not so long ago, I wasn't so sure it was ever going to happen for me. When I marched into his office last month, full of rage about not being promoted yet, he came back at me with his typical, soft-spoken tone. But, what he said was pretty hard to take.

"Penelope, please close the door and sit down. We need to discuss this a little bit."

I know, right? Nothing good ever follows words like that.

Away from work, he would have definitely tossed a *darlin'* or a *honey* in there somewhere, but he never does that at the office. I've always admired his ability to keep work and the fact that he's basically been a second father to me for my entire life completely separate. He's a great man.

I was more than just a little bit stunned when he wanted me to close the door. He took away all of my steam in less than five seconds and I actually thought I was about to be fired.

I slowed my roll instantly and then sat in the chair in front of his desk. I fidgeted like a schoolgirl in the principal's office who was waiting to hear that she's about to have detention for the next couple of afternoons.

"People here have been complaining about you. They say you think you're smarter than everyone else and you never listen to anyone's opinions about anything."

I looked at the ceiling and resisted the urge to roll my eyes.

Mr. Milan picked up a piece of paper and started reading from it out loud. "I've been here for thirteen years and she obviously thinks I have no idea what I'm talking about. Don't get me wrong, she's good at what she does, but so am I. It would be nice if my boss thought so too."

He stopped and looked at me. I just shrugged and gave him an awkward smile. I had no idea what to say about that.

Mr. Milan picked up another piece of paper and read that one aloud. "Every time I go to talk to her about something she's very short with me. She acts like she can't wait for me to stop speaking and just leave her alone."

Again, I didn't know what to say, so I sat there and remained silent.

I could feel myself shrinking in one of Mr. Milan's visitor's' chairs. I felt like a child who was about to be sent to her room for a timeout, but one who felt really sorry for whatever she'd done. I may have even thought about crying for a second. But I didn't.

Once I had stopped myself from crying, I could feel myself getting angry. What the heck were these people trying to do to me? I am not this person that they're describing. Or am I?

"Do you have anything to add, Miss Pym?"

Miss Pym? He's never, ever called me that. Not away from work or at work. I suspected his next comment would include the words, *you're fired.*

"Sometimes people mistake my being a quiet person for me thinking I'm better than they are. It's like they think I'm feeling too good about myself to speak with them. It's been that way for my entire life. I can try to..."

"Is that all?"

"I'm not arrogant, Mr. Milan. I can't change my demeanor. I can't be super social all the time. People just read me wrong—like, all the time. I'm not sure how to please these people."

So, we went back and forth like that for a little while longer. Shockingly, I didn't get fired. I kind of feel like I should have been now that I think about it all a little more.

Instead of sending me packing, Mr. Milan gave me an assignment. Well, he kind of changed the rules on one I was already working on.

The company was just about to get started on making this new line of markers for golf balls. You know, when your ball is on the green, but you pick it up so someone farther away from the hole can shoot before you?

We make these flat ball markers so your ball is out of their way when the other person shoots. You put your marker down and then you know where to put your ball back when it's your turn.

I'm sorry if you already knew all of that. To be honest, I didn't, but I've never played golf in my life. Maybe I should start—considering where I work and all.

My job as an operations manager was to coordinate the new product line. I had to line up the work centers in our system properly, work with the engineers to create the proper lead times for materials and manufacturing, communicate all of that to our sales team, and then off we would go with production—when that time came.

I'd known about the new line for a few weeks, and already had most of that worked out. But, Mr. Milan had this new idea.

"I want you to delegate every part of setting up that product line down to your team. You can answer any questions they have, but they're doing all of the work. I mean it. They handle it all."

"But I've already started..."

"Miss Pym. If you can get through this little experiment successfully, we'll talk about your promotion. That's all I've got for you right now. You need to get your team together and let them know what we need from them."

So, that was about six weeks ago, and guess what? I know, you already know. I got the promotion.

I have to admit, I hated what Mr. Milan was asking me to do when he asked me to do it. This meant that I had to throw away everything I had already worked on and allow this group of traitors to do it instead. And I couldn't just tell them to do it my way.

Oh, and I also had to walk on egg shells so they wouldn't write any more love notes to Mr. Milan about me.

Turns out, they did a pretty good job. Some of the ideas were even better than mine—some of them.

During the process, my people were so happy about the trust I had shown them, that I actually converted a couple of them from enemies to friends. I even went out with them and the rest of the crew to have drinks last night.

I went out on a Thursday night with my coworkers. Who knew that was ever going to happen? Yeah, I know, Mr. Milan knew.

Thank God, he didn't fire me.

I realize there's nothing about Evan in this entry, but since the promotion was such a big chunk of my last entry, along with Evan's bombshell, I figured it was necessary to close the loop on that part of the memoir.

From the moment I was forced to trust my coworkers, things improved dramatically for me at work. Not only did I get the promotion to Operations Manager, but I had begun to understand the importance of treating my coworkers like equals. We started to form some powerful bonds.

I didn't just begin to change at work. Mr. Milan's little experiment helped me to realize how my attitude was making it extremely difficult for people to approach me. What I'm saying—what I was so reluctant to admit back then—is that I had a major attitude problem. Everyone seemed to know that except me.

While I do still believe that I'm a fairly intelligent person, I no longer believe everyone else is clueless. And while I recognize that people will inevitably make a mistake or two, a mistake doesn't mean a person is completely incompetent.

I do openly admit that I still have trouble owning up to my own mistakes—sometimes.

What can I say? I'm a perpetual work in progress.

Chapter 15

March 17, 2016

Dear Diary,

Happy Saint Patrick's Day! Mr. Milan actually closed the office early today and joined us for our weekly Thursday night social hour. It's rare that he comes out with us, but he does—sometimes. I have to say, he's never closed the office early for it. And he's not even Irish.

I've had more than two green beers. Two is my typical limit on beers, or anything with alcohol, but we did get off to an early start today. Allow me to apologize in advance if this goes astray.

Something extremely unexpected happened last weekend and I've been a little too busy to tell you all about it. I'm pretty sure that even you won't believe me when I finally do get to the actual point.

What was I about to tell you? Oh, yeah, I had a most unexpected visitor on Sunday.

Scarlett came to my apartment. I know, right? The one and only backstabbing nuisance of a former best friend actually came knocking at my door on a Sunday afternoon.

I almost didn't open the door when I saw her face through the little peep-hole thingy. It's been YEARS since we've had any meaningful social contact.

I stared at her for a while through the peep hole. She looked sad out there. She had a bottle of wine and this look on her face—like she knew I was here, but she wasn't sure if I would actually answer the door or not.

I almost didn't. Did I mention that?

I finally opened up and asked her to come in. I wanted to be rude to her, but I also wanted to give her a hug. It was the strangest feeling. It felt similar to when I'm around Evan and I can't decide if I want to kiss him or punch him—or kiss him and then punch him.

It was like that with Scarlett and a hug—but no punch. I think Scarlett would thoroughly enjoy beating the crap out of me. So, the toughest thing I would be brave enough to do to her is blow her off with a smile.

Scarlett told me she had something really important to talk with me about, so we sat at my tiny little two-person dining room table and she got right to it.

"Evan needs you to tell him how you feel. He's miserable and he's driving everyone around him nuts. He's never gonna come to you and try again. It's on you now."

Wait, what? Try what again? I thought all of that—I didn't say anything. I just looked at Scarlett with a confused face. I maybe even tilted my head a little like a puppy when someone starts speaking to it.

"He came to you and spilled his guts. He told you that he was in love with you and you just kind of shrugged it off, like he was giving you a weather report or something. He confessed his love for you."

I was really confused about what she was telling me. I did a little math on my fingers and replied, "That was like, nine months ago. He barely even speaks to me anymore. Even when he comes to see his dad at work, he never stops by to say hi."

"He's afraid to talk to you. Why didn't you just tell him the truth? We all know it. We've always known it. You two are in love with each other. You've been in love with each other since preschool for crying out loud."

I resisted the urge to remind Scarlett that she dated him while she was one of the *we all* who knew it. I was still confused about what she expected me to do and I wanted her to clarify all of that.

"Penelope, you need to tell him. I can't deal with him at work. He's not himself. He's kind of a jerk lately, if I'm being honest."

"Oh, you mean Evan can be a jerk? There's a real shocker. I suppose you think that's my fault?"

"Do you even know him anymore? Evan is the nicest person I know. The things he's done for his employees—the things he's done for me. Evan is great man. His employees worship him."

"Everyone in Pella worships Evan. He's that super good-looking football star from yesteryear. People have worshipped Evan since the day he was born. They worship his whole family."

"Whatever. Just trust me for once. I'm trying to do you and him a huge favor. I care about Evan. He's my best friend. And whether you believe it or not, I care about you too. If you listen to me, you can thank me when you're happily married."

We talked for a little while longer, and even had a glass of the wine she brought. For a minute I didn't hate her. Maybe it was less than a minute. Maybe it was ten seconds—I don't remember right now.

I walked her to the door and gave her that hug I was talking about before.

I know. It was a moment of weakness—she was actually being really sweet though.

Before she got too far down the hall outside my door she turned around. "You promise me that you're gonna go and see him. Real soon, Penelope."

I closed my eyes and took a deep breath. "I promise."

Why did I make that promise?

I know. Now I gotta go see Evan and tell him how I feel. That's not gonna be too awkward at all, right?

Question—do you actually have to keep a promise that you make to a snake?

It was Scarlett, the girl who I had sworn to hate for the rest of my life, who made that final push to get Evan and me on the same page romantically.

Though she had messed up all those years before, she really did care about us—both of us. Coming to see me out of the blue, knowing I was more likely to slam the door in her face than to invite her in, proved it.

Scarlett was right about Evan's employees loving him. He was a lot like his father in that regard, except Scarlett had explained something to me that night that made me believe he was even more generous than Mr. Milan.

Evan's business, like any landscaping company, hired a lot of young part-timers during the summer months when he was insanely busy. But, when his part-timers left during the slow winter months—some without a lot of options—Evan not only encouraged them to go to college, he helped to pay for their tuition.

Evan's company had even paid entire tuition costs for a couple of his employees who would otherwise have never been able to go to college. Scarlett told me that the first employee that Evan put through college was her.

Once Scarlett was done with school, the two of them continued the same practice with more of his employees. Scarlett even helped with applications and financial aid paperwork. Those who couldn't get into a state university were encouraged to go to a local community college.

The company also gave huge cash bonuses for good grades—high school or college.

Word got out about what Evan's landscaping company was doing for the community, and business got pretty good, pretty quickly. Businesses in town were lining up to hire him for their landscaping and snow removal needs.

I'd always known that Evan was good man, but until Scarlett's unexpected visit, I had no idea how good. I'd been crushing on him since I was in pigtails, so I knew he had some great qualities—despite being a bit of a player who was far too self-aware of his charm and good looks—but I didn't know he was an actual prince.

After Scarlett left my apartment, I knew that I wanted to go and see Evan as quickly as possible. I had to let him know that I felt the same way. I was actually super excited about the prospect of finally doing so.

Even though I was reassured by one of his closest friends that he wanted me to come to him—he was dying for me to come to him—I still trembled at the idea of actually doing it.

Chapter 16

April 1, 2016

Dear Diary,

It's April Fool's Day and a Friday night. I'm sitting here, alone, hoping that I haven't done something terribly foolish. I'm also hoping that maybe I won't have to spend many more Friday nights by myself. I guess time will tell.

It took a couple weeks, but I finally took Scarlett's advice and had that long-overdue talk with Evan. It happened in my office today, right before lunch.

Evan showed up to meet with Mr. Milan for their typical lunch together. They're still doing that at least once or twice a week—it's very sweet. I spotted him waiting and asked him to come and see me for a quick chat. Mr. Milan was on a call or trying to finish up with something—or whatever—he was busy. Evan shrugged and followed me.

He had this look on his face like he really didn't want to be there when he came into my office. I almost chickened out, but I had promised myself like three times that no matter what he said, or how he looked at me, I would tell him the truth—finally. I refused to fail this time.

Evan walked in closely behind me and I gently grabbed his arm while I reached around him to close the door. He looked at my hand and smiled at me. My fears melted instantly.

Evan has this way of making you feel great with just one smile. Thank goodness he did, because before he smiled at me, I was shaking in my flats. I was fraught with doubt and wondering if I was about to embarrass myself horribly.

Before I started talking, I had this odd thought. *What if he's seeing someone?*

He and I weren't talking—we hadn't been for months. I had no idea if he was dating someone or not. Logic would suggest that Scarlett wouldn't have come and told me to make a move if he was—or would she have?

"Should I sit down, Pen?" Evan asked. He still had that make-you-feel-amazing smile on his face. This was starting out a lot better than I had hoped.

"I think you should."

"Oh my. What's on your mind?"

"Evan, I owe you an apology. You came in here all those months ago and laid your feelings out in the open. And then I just kind of shrugged you off. I regret doing that to you. I'm sorry."

"You don't have to say you're sorry. I get it. You don't feel the same way. I'm a big boy, Pen. I can take it."

I wanted to start yelling at him for saying that after he had basically ignored me for nine months.

Can you take it? Where have you been? But I knew if I did that that it would defeat the entire purpose of your little private meeting. He might have stormed off and not spoken to me for another nine months—maybe longer.

No. Let it go, Penelope.

It was time to fix our friendship, and maybe even start something more. It was time to stop letting distractions get in our way. I needed to focus and say what I had promised myself I would say.

"We both know that's not true. You must know that's not true, right?"

"I'm not sure what you're asking me here. It is true. I can handle it if you don't feel the same way about me that I do for you. I've just been trying to move on, Pen. That's why I've been avoiding you. I can't believe you're actually…"

"Evan! I *do* feel the same way. I've been madly in love with you for as long as I can remember. Geez, Evan. You're so dumb sometimes."

I probably shouldn't have added that last part, but I couldn't help myself. You remember what I told you before? It's that kiss-him-or-punch-him thing. He makes me confused like that all the time.

"I didn't know. I'm sorry. You have no idea how hard it is to read you sometimes. Why didn't you just tell me?"

"I'm telling you right now. If it's not too late, I think you and I should stop all of this avoiding each other."

I was back to shaking. Evan had this blank look on his face and he kept looking away from me. He was staring at the top of my desk for an eternity and I couldn't take it anymore.

"Aren't you gonna say something?" I asked. It was the same question he had asked me all those months ago when he told me how he felt and I just froze.

Was it my turn to suffer?

He took forever to change his expression and then forever again to finally speak. I was terrified that he was about to turn and walk away without saying anything, like he did last time.

And then the smile returned to his beautiful face. Instant relief. Speak, Evan. Speak.

"What are you doing tomorrow night?"

Finally. In case it wasn't clear, the last line of my diary entry was Evan asking me out on our very first date. I had kind of expected a positive reaction from him, given what Scarlett had told me, but I had no idea things would happen so quickly.

After I had agreed to go out with him, Evan and I planned a pretty simple night out in Pella. He met me at my apartment and we walked from there past the Vermeer Windmill and through Central Park to a Mexican restaurant on Washington Street.

There are plenty of upscale places we could have gone to in Pella, but neither of us has ever been into that sort of thing. We like to keep it simple.

Even though it was our first date, we agreed to nothing fancy. For me, I love Pella so much in the spring that I consider a walk through downtown in April to be nothing short of amazing. I didn't need fancy overpriced food to dress it up. The company I was with was pretty great too.

How to describe Pella in the spring? The annual Tulip Festival was only a few weeks away on the night of our first date, and though the thousands of tulips planted all over town were not in full bloom just yet, the scenery was breathtaking—as always.

The Vermeer Windmill is this gigantic Dutch-style windmill that was actually built in the Netherlands and shipped to Pella in 2002. I had mentioned early in this memoir that Pella was America's Dutch Treasure. Well, almost every small town in the Netherlands has a mill at its center. And, since 2002, so does Pella.

She's a true beauty, but I've always pictured her in a field of red tulips in the countryside in Holland, instead of in the middle of downtown on Franklin Street. I'm not complaining. I absolutely love the Vermeer Windmill.

Evan and I walked through Central Park holding hands. There's another windmill there as well—we have a total of five Dutch windmills in Pella. There were tulips in gardens all over Central Park and lining the sidewalks—not in full bloom yet, but still beautiful. Central Park in Pella is probably my favorite place on planet Earth.

There are a few other popular Pella landmarks in the park to go with all the tulip gardens. There's the Sundial, which was gifted to Pella from Heritage Lace, Inc. in 1991. It's a beautiful steel structure that serves as a time piece and symbol of unity and celebration.

You can't help but notice the Tulip Tower. It's a sixty-five-feet tall structure with the words *Tulip Time* at the top. A temporary tower was first put up in 1940 for the Tulip Festival, and it was so popular that it was re-erected every year. Eventually, in 1968, a permanent tower was built.

I considered showing Evan my bench. Well, it's not my bench, but every Saturday morning at ten o'clock, I walk to the Brew House on Franklin Street, buy a spiced chai latte, and settle on the same bench in Central Park for a couple of hours to read a book.

I led Evan over to my bench, but stopped short of letting him in on my nerdy little Saturday ritual. He was the town's favorite super jock after all. Would he find it silly? Besides, if he had a negative reaction, I would have been crushed—our first date may have been our last.

I stopped us right in front of my bench and tried to think of something clever to say. To me this was a special place, but I didn't know how to tell Evan that.

"Why are stopping here?" he asked.

"I just wanted to take a second to take it all in. I love this spot more than any other place."

Right about the time I started to feel just a little embarrassed about stopping us at a bench, when we were surrounded by extremely popular and beautiful town landmarks, *Mr. Super Jock* himself leaned in and we shared our first kiss.

"Pen, you're amazing. I've been wanting to do that for longer than you'll ever know."

Oh, I knew. I absolutely knew.

I smiled at him and punched him softly on the chest.

"Um, ouch. What the heck was that for?"

"Oh, no reason."

I didn't have the heart to tell him that I'd always imagined myself kissing him, or punching him, or kissing him and then punching him. I suppose he knows that now.

For the record, our first kiss was even better than I had ever imagined. In fact, our first date, though quite simple, had exceeded all expectations.

Oh, and Evan had already known about my Saturday spot in Central Park. I found out later that he'd seen me there many times, but he didn't want to disturb me while I was reading—at least that's what he told me.

Chapter 17

April 1, 2017

Dear Diary,

Exactly one year ago today, I confessed my love for Evan. That is, on April Fool's Day, I declared myself a fool for the most amazing person in my life.

Consequently, since that lovely fool's day, my life has never been better. We're both so happy. My only regret, if it can even be considered one, is that it took me so long to figure out how perfect we would be together.

Well, if you had eyes, which you obviously do not, you probably would have noticed a beautiful and sparkly little rock on the ring finger of my left hand.

That's right. Evan asked me to marry him this morning. I said yes, clearly, and, just like that, I am engaged to the absolute love of my life.

We spent the day with all four of our parents, celebrating the occasion. They already knew it was going to happen, so they planned out a nice dinner date for the six of us.

Good thing I said yes, don't you think? I know—yeah, right. There was absolutely no chance of the word *no* entering my brain or leaving my lips while Evan was kneeling before me with this beautiful ring in his hand.

I must confess, the way he proposed, today—on April Fool's Day—was probably the most romantic, and also hilarious thing that has ever happened to me.

You're gonna love this.

So, considering that today is Saturday, I'm sure you know exactly where I was at ten o'clock this morning.

You guessed it. I was on my bench, reading.

Even though I've been spending a ton of time with Evan lately, I have most certainly not given up my Saturday mornings in Central Park with a book. Besides, Evan works most Saturdays—

like all day long—so I still have a lot of free time on Saturday mornings.

Well on this particular Saturday—April Fool's Day and all—our adorable, scheming Evan took the day off and snuck into the park to wait for me.

There I was, reading my copy of *The Girl on the Train,* by Paula Hawkins, blissfully unaware of what was happening around me. I heard the plane—it was actually pretty loud—but I chose to completely ignore the distraction. That book is really, really good.

I continued reading and then I heard a familiar voice.

"Look up. Look up, now!"

I'm sure whoever that annoying person is, they're not talking to me, I thought, and I continued reading.

"Look up! Penelope Pym! For the love of God, look up!"

That got my attention.

I looked up, and there, flying low in the clear blue sky, I spotted a plane dragging one of those advertisement signs. You know, the kind you see at State Fairs or other events with big outdoor crowds.

Apparently, the plane had already passed in the sky directly in front of me once, and it was turning around to make another pass. I watched as it circled back.

And then, as it got a little closer, I was able to read the sign. "Pen Pym will you marry me?"

I sat there, looking up, feeling completely stunned for about three minutes—three minutes that felt like an eternity. And then Evan gently tapped me on the leg and brought me out of my trance.

He was down on one knee with this enormous smile on his face. He had the ring in his hand and extended it to me.

I just froze with my mouth open, trying to catch flies, I guess. I couldn't speak.

"Well, will ya?"

I still don't know exactly how I feel about Evan's choice of April Fool's Day as the day he decided to propose to me, but everything else was absolutely perfect. Lucky for me, the proposal was not an April Fool's joke.

It was on that day, one year earlier, that I had chosen to tell him that I was in love with him. And he proposed at the same location where we had our first kiss. So, seeing that I'm at least partially to blame for the setting of Evan's grand gesture, I shouldn't complain.

Maybe April Fool's Day is the most appropriate day, considering how long it took for both of us to see what everyone around us had been seeing for our entire lives. We've certainly taken a day meant for pranks and turned it into our own magical day. I guess that's a blessing for both of us.

I don't think the proposal could have been more perfect. I laugh every time I think about Evan lurking somewhere in Central Park, in an absolute panic as I completely ignored the first pass of the plane.

The pilot was one of his friends who does crop dusting and occasionally flies around with advertisement banners. I'm sure Evan would have had him back in the sky at some point if I had missed their first attempt. Would he have waited for the next April Fool's Day to fall on a Saturday? I sure hope not.

"For the love of God, look up!"

Absolutely hilarious.

That moment not only provides us both with an amazing memory, it also gave us a catch phrase to use every single time we have an argument. One of us simply tells the other to *look up*. It's our little reminder to stop what we're doing and think. It's our cue to let the argument die and remember how much we love each other. And it ends any frustration either of us is feeling toward the other—instantly.

We don't argue much, but we have our fair share of disagreements. We're definitely two very different people, but that works for us—and it works quite well.

Evan is still everyone in Pella's best friend. He's the life of the party—he's constantly the center of attention. I'm still the person least likely to speak or stand out in a crowd.

Lucky for me, Evan handles all of that for both of us. Yet, in spite of it all, he's never made me feel left behind—not once. He's very good at understanding how I dread being in a crowd. He constantly looks out for me to make sure that I haven't retreated to some quiet place away from it all. He never lets me feel left out.

Though I never, ever want to be the center of attention, I get a kick out of seeing Evan among our friends and family. He has this energy that he loves to share with everyone in the room. And they absolutely love to gobble it up. So, for my part, I make sure that I don't take him away from those moments. He deserves them and he thoroughly enjoys them.

We're far from perfect. And like I said, we argue sometimes. But we always come back to the same place together. We're so lucky to have our *look up* memory. That lovely little gesture is still incredibly effective in ending every disagreement. Let's hope we continue to carry it with us for a long and happy marriage.

Our promise to each other is to start and end every day with a hug and a kiss—and sometimes, the kiss might be followed with a gentle punch to Evan's chest.

I have to say, the soft punch will likely be my favorite of our little traditions.

Chapter 18

October 5, 2018

My Dearest, Evan,

Thislast chapter is for you, my love. What a journey we've shared together. And the very best days are obviously yet to come. I look forward to being your wife and sharing the rest of my life with you.

I've completely lost count of the number of times that I've cried while writing this memoir. Happy tears, all of them. I've probably burst out laughing more than a dozen times as well.

I can't wait to see your reaction when you read it. Will it make you cry? Will it make you laugh? Will it make you change your mind about us? Surely, I don't believe it will.

Though I've only chosen seventeen actual diary entries to add to this memoir, trust me, there are perhaps a hundred more that tell our story. I cherry-picked the very best and most interesting.

Besides, who wants to take a deep dive into the mind of a confused and often angry young woman? I'll admit in earnest, I definitely do not.

I'm sure that you and perhaps the most observant readers—should we allow anyone else to actually read this—will notice that there are no diary entries listed in this memoir between the day you and I started dating and the day you proposed to me.

I know I had promised to include all of the most interesting entries that had something to do with telling our story. And I know that I've included some pretty personal information about myself and my most cherished friends. But some moments in our story are meant to be kept private.

Besides, my love, our moms and dads will probably be reading this.

I had to leave at least a few things for our eyes only. I promise, if you ever want to read those entries leading up to your proposal, they're all yours, babe. The entire diary is an open book, should you decide to take a more in-depth peek.

I'll leave you and anyone else who has actually gotten this far along in the reading with this—I am marrying the man who I believe that God has made just for me, we're ridiculously happy together, and I'm no longer known exclusively as *The Powerful Penelope Pym*.

I'm also the luckiest woman alive.

Acknowledgments

Thank you to my wife, Renee, and my kids, Emily and Austin. You encourage and inspire me to keep going every day. Thank you for allowing me to pursue my dream and for giving me more than enough support to keep it alive. I love you all so very much.

It's become common practice for me to put some form of art on the page just before the start of my books. For this one, it's the page opposite the preface. The printers like to keep that page blank, but I prefer to dress it up a little.

I tried something a little different for that art this time around. I went to someone I'd never worked with before and asked for a digital design instead of an actual painting on a canvas. Thank you to Kashaf Mehsania of Internative Labs for the illustration of the Vermeer Windmill. You captured my vision, and Penelope's, perfectly. We both truly appreciate the effort.

Thanks, once again, to Dennis Kouba for helping me to make my words more readable. We've worked together on a few of my books and I swear that I learn something new and improve every time we collaborate. I really appreciate that.

I'd like to acknowledge the beautiful city of Pella, Iowa. Thank you for the inspiration. Pella comes complete with authentic Dutch windmills, lots of tulips, and many, many other lovely surprises. I will most likely never be moving away from New England, but I sure wouldn't mind spending some time in Pella.

How did Penelope Pym get her name? I'm happy to acknowledge the two amazing authors who inspired it. A very special thank you to the late Penelope Mortimer and Barbara Pym.

Penelope Mortimer was a bit ahead of her time as a feminist before the world—or at least most of the world—was ready for feminism. Her worked gained popularity and created controversy in the 1950s and beyond. And though her work was quite extraordinary, it remains largely unknown—which is a shame for all of us.

I would encourage anyone to look up *A Villa in Summer, Daddy's Gone A-Hunting,* or *The Pumpkin Eater.*

Barbara Pym also made her mark in the 1950's and beyond. She wasn't as controversial a figure as Mortimer, but her work has also tragically been forgotten and revived, and then forgotten and revived again. Pym, like Mortimer, has tragically and inexplicably not received the recognition she deserves. Perhaps daring to challenge the status quo of 1950's society was too much for the literary world to bear. But I think we can handle it now.

Some of Pym's more popular work includes, *Excellent Women, Quartet in Autumn,* and *A Glass of Blessings.*

Also by Brian D. Campbell

The Third King: Coronation
Part I of the Ben Gilsum Book Series
(Red Cliff Press, 2018)

Guardian Angel: True Calling
Part II of the Ben Gilsum Book Series
(Red Cliff Press, 2019)

Denying The Stylus
A Novella by Brian D. Campbell
(Red Cliff Press, 2020)

The Center Bench All-Star
(Red Cliff Press, 2021)

The Silver Rain
(Red Cliff Press, 2023)

For More Information

Visit our website:
www.redcliffpress.wordpress.com